C

Black Pearl
Ponies

The BLACK PEARL PONIES series:

Black Pearl Ponies

WILD*f*LOWER

JENNY OLDFIELD

Illustrated by
JOHN GREEN

Hodder
Children's
Books

A division of Hachette Children's Books

A Catalogue record for this book is available from the British Library

ISBN 978 0 340 99893 9

Printed and bound in the UK by
CPI Bookmarque Ltd, Croydon, CR0 4TD

The paper and board used in this paperback by
Hodder Children's Books are natural recyclable products made from wood
grown in sustainable forests. The manufacturing processes conform to the
environmental regulations of the country of origin.

Hodder Children's Books
A division of Hachette Children's Books
338 Euston Road, London NW1 3BH
An Hachette UK company
www.hachette.co.uk

Once more with thanks to the Foster family and all my friends at Lost Valley Ranch, and this time with special thanks to Katie Foster, horse trainer and all-round equine expert.

CHAPTER ONE

'Red Star, look at this!' Keira Lucas pinned up a big, shiny photograph of the two of them on the stable wall. It showed her and her pony winning their prize at the recent County competition.

Red Star looked up from his bucket of grain pellets and snickered.

'Come over here and look!' she insisted.

The strawberry roan pony sighed and then joined

her. He nuzzled Keira's cheek as he peered over her shoulder.

'That's us at the Sheriton show,' she told him. 'There's Smoky, the winner of the reining competition, with his owner, Scott Newsome. And that's us beside them, taking second prize.'

The pony stared hard at the picture then turned his head to Keira with what seemed like a questioning look.

'Yeah, next time we'll definitely come in first!' she promised with a laugh. 'But you did great, Red Star. All those sliding stops were perfect. It was only one faulty lead change that lost us points.'

Keira remembered happily the day two weeks earlier when the whole family – herself, her sister, Brooke, and her mom and dad had got in the truck and trailered Red Star over to Sheriton. She recalled how excited she'd been, waiting to ride her pony into the arena, then the thrill of riding in front of a huge crowd, and the pride she'd felt when they'd all clapped and cheered.

Red Star had looked perfect – ears pricked and head held high, silken white mane and tail flowing, his speckled red-grey coat brushed to a high sheen. And he'd totally enjoyed every second of his time in the arena.

'Not bad for a first effort,' Keira's mom, Allyson, had said afterwards.

'Not bad? That was amazing!' her dad, Jacob, had said.

And they'd gone into Sheriton for a family pizza to celebrate before they'd trailered Red Star home to Black Pearl Ranch.

It was late October and the days were drawing in, the nights growing colder, which meant they brought the ponies into the barn at night and gave them feed. Each morning they put them out into the meadow beside the creek.

'It's OK – you can go back and eat now!' Keira said, laughing as Red Star snorted and went to stick his head in the feed bucket.

'I see you taught him to speak English!' Jacob Lucas grinned as he led his grey mare, Misty, into the stable opposite Red Star's. Along the row, other ponies stuck their heads over their stable doors, including the two brood mares, Ruby and Willow.

'Red Star is the smartest pony around!' Keira insisted. She smoothed out the picture then came out of the stable and bolted the door.

'And the best looking!' her dad kidded. 'Plus, he's the best cow pony, the best barrel racer, the best ...'

'I'm serious. He's just the best!' And Keira marched off with a grin, down the dimly lit central aisle, past the high stack of hay bales and the grain store, out into the corral where a thin silver moon shone bright in a star-studded sky.

That night clouds came in over Black Pearl Mountains and next morning there was snow on the ground.

Keira got up early and went down to the kitchen, drawn by the smell of bacon cooking and the sound of eggs frying in the pan.

'Who wants to drive with me out to Norton County?' Allyson asked. 'I'm giving a follow-up riding lesson to Meredith Mason and Tornado.'

'Me. I'll come.' Brooke was quick to offer, even though she was still in her pyjamas, her dark hair uncombed.

'That means you steer clear of Saturday chores,' Keira grumbled. She knew they couldn't both go – her dad would need help here.

'OK, you do it,' Brooke sniffed. 'I don't care.'

'No, actually. I want to work with Dad on the new filly.'

'So stay.'

'Girls!' Allyson broke in. 'Whoever comes, you need to be ready to leave in ten minutes.'

'You go with Mom this week, I'll go next,' Keira said finally. As Brooke ran upstairs to get dressed, Keira began to list in her head the chores she needed to finish before she got to go in the arena with her dad. Clean the tack, sweep out the tack room, feed the ponies, lead them out into the snowy meadow – and all this before she helped her dad with the filly.

'Remember the farrier's due at noon,' Allyson reminded Jacob and Keira as she drained her coffee cup.

'Add it to the list,' Jacob told Keira. 'So why are we sitting around talking? We have work to do!'

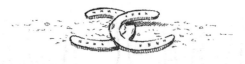

'It's always like this,' Keira told Ruby and Willow's two spring foals as she led them out into the

meadow. 'At Black Pearl Ranch we work, work, work!'

Spider and Toots high-stepped on their spindly legs, lifting their tiny hooves clear of the snow. Spider was Willow's dark bay baby – a foal with a pretty face topped by a tufty black mane. His legs were so long they seemed to go on forever. Toots belonged to Ruby. Like her mom, she was a beautiful sorrel with a white star on her forehead.

'It's OK, I know you've never seen snow,' Keira laughed as the foals hung back at the meadow gate. 'It's just frozen rain. It's not going to hurt you!'

Toots and Spider lowered their heads and sniffed the white stuff. They gave tiny snorts when the cold powder touched their noses, then they looked up with puzzled expressions.

'Go!' Keira told them, holding the gate open.

From across the meadow, Ruby and Willow neighed.

At last the foals decided it was safe and they broke into jerky canters to join their moms by the feed rack.

This left Keira free to work with her dad. Going back to the barn, she took Red Star from his stable and walked him into the corral. 'No saddle and bridle today,' she explained. 'I won't be riding you 'cos Dad needs you in the arena.'

OK, whatever, Red Star seemed to say, walking steadily beside her and waiting for her to open the arena gate. Inside the round pen, Jacob was already at work.

'This is Sasha.' Keira introduced Red Star to the

two-year-old colt. 'She belongs to a guy named Jim Peynton. Jim has asked Dad to break her in ready for his son to ride.'

Red Star snickered and nodded. He walked straight across to the nervous youngster.

'Hey, Red Star,' Jacob said quietly. He'd spent a few minutes with Sasha, running his hands over her neck and back, getting her used to him being around. Then he'd laid a saddle across her back for the very first time. 'Your job is to tell her the saddle's fine – no need to freak out.'

Keira's pony stepped right in to the task. He nuzzled Sasha's cheek and took a good sniff at the saddle, walked all around her then invited her to take a walk with him around the snow-covered arena. Sasha followed, stepping where he stepped, shadowing his every move.

Jacob nodded. 'Time to slip a bit into her mouth,' he decided, handing the bit and bridle to his daughter. 'You do it, Keira.'

'Cool!' She was pleased that her dad trusted her with some important work. 'Here, baby, this bit might feel weird 'cos it's cold and shiny, but Red Star wears one all the time.' Carefully and very gently Keira slipped her fingers into Sasha's mouth and eased in the bit. As soon as it was in over her tongue, she buckled on the bridle.

The filly's ears went back flat against her head. *What's this? What are you doing to me?*

Again Red Star stepped in with a few soft nuzzles to soothe the colt's nerves.

'Good job, Red Star,' Jacob murmured before he

looked over the corral to see that a visitor had arrived. 'Here's Reed,' he told Keira. 'Let's leave these two in the round pen while we find out what he wants.'

CHAPTER TWO

'If you can get a horse to love you, she'll do anything for you,' Jacob told Reed Walters. He, Reed and Keira were standing in the corral next to Wildflower, Reed's new Appaloosa pony. 'She'll even die for you.'

'I hear you, Mr Lucas,' Reed replied. He said he'd ridden Wildflower along Low Ridge from his home at the Three Horseshoes – his first outing with the nervy three-year-old.

'She's pretty!' Keira sighed. She stood back to admire the Appie's chocolate-brown and white markings, the dark mane and tail.

'It's all about getting them to accept you,' Jacob insisted. 'Like little Sasha in there – you have to be gentle with them and build up the trust.'

Reed was only half listening. 'I spoke with

Brooke earlier. Wildflower needs shoes and she told me you've got the farrier here today.'

'Soon,' Keira told him, glancing down to see that Wildflower was currently without a set of shoes. 'Where did you buy Wildflower? And what happened to Duke?'

'Duke is semi-retired,' Reed explained. 'He's an old guy now, and Dad said he'd buy me something new.'

'Poor old Duke,' Keira sighed. She'd hate it if the time ever came to retire Red Star, and she was sure she wouldn't do it so carelessly. But twelve-year-old boys were different, she thought. On the surface, they didn't show so much love for their ponies – which was why her dad was doing the straight talking with Reed.

'What's Wildflower's history?' Jacob asked.

'We bought her from my dad's rancher buddy in Texas.'

'And you wanted an Appaloosa?'

'Yeah, I like a challenge,' Reed said. 'Something with gas in its tank.'

A pony is not a car engine! Keira thought with a frown.

'So long as she listens,' Jacob warned. 'Speed is cool, but only if she doesn't ignore you and ride through the bit.'

As they were talking, Wildflower stood hyper-alert, taking in her surroundings. Her ears flicked, she turned her head this way and that. When Keira tried to stroke her neck, she shifted nervously out of reach.

But wow, she was beautiful, Keira decided – lightly built, with that wonderful dark-chocolate and whipped-cream colouring and those big dark brown eyes.

'She'll be cool once I've put some miles on her,' Reed insisted.

'And come to me if you have problems,' Jacob offered.

'Thanks, Mr Lucas, I'll remember that,' came the awkward reply.

For some reason Keira felt uneasy too. She was glad when she heard a truck bumping over the rough dirt track and she turned to see that it was the farrier, Jeff Taylor, driving in across the cattle guard.

Jeff was a broad-shouldered man with a big,

dark moustache. He wore a huge leather apron and a wide belt loaded with tools. He whistled while he worked. Against a background of rhythmic hammering, Keira heard a tune she recognised about blue Colorado skies.

'Your turn next,' she told Red Star as Jeff finished work on Captain's shoes and led him out of the stall.

The farrier handed Captain over to Jacob then called Keira across. She took her pony into the stall and stood with him as Jeff lifted his feet and jerked nails out of his old shoes with a big pair of pliers. He rasped each of Red Star's hooves then went to his van to fetch new shoes, his whistle mingling with the ring of metal.

'Quit that!' Reed said sharply to Wildflower as the young Appie reared up on the end of her lead rope. They were standing last in line and it was clear that Wildflower was not looking forward to being led into the farrier's stall.

'The noises spook her,' Keira decided. 'Has she had shoes before?'

'Who knows?' Reed replied. 'But she sure needs them around here. We ride on rough territory out at the Three Horseshoes.'

Tap-tap-tap – Jeff's hammer drove the nails into

Red Star's feet.

Wildflower reared again and tried to back away.

Tap-tap! The farrier finished with Red Star and asked Keira to back him out.

'Good boy,' she murmured. 'We're done.'

'OK, let's go.' Reed made as if to move into the stall with Wildflower. 'I said, let's go,' he insisted as the Appie braced her front legs and refused to move.

Jeff frowned and looked at his watch. 'I don't have time to wait until she decides she's ready,' he warned.

Reed sighed and pulled at the lead rope.

'Hey, that's nine-hundred pounds of solid muscle on the end of that rope,' Jacob pointed out. 'Brute strength won't cut it with her.'

By now there was no way Wildflower would co-operate. She was tugging back, her ears were flat against her head and she rolled her eyes to show the whites. Watching from a safe distance, Keira saw Reed lose the tug of war and watched Wildflower back up right against the side of Jeff's van – which was when the pony spooked big time.

Crash! Wildflower lashed out with her hind feet

and kicked the side of the van with full force. There was a loud, dull thud, a big dent and a couple of swear words from Jeff Taylor. Wildflower rocked back on her haunches and launched herself forward, tearing the lead rope clean out of Reed's hands.

Then she was galloping round the arena, rope trailing in the dirty, churned-up snow, looking for an escape route.

'Forget it,' Jeff grunted as he began to stack his tools into the van. 'Reed, you find yourself another farrier for that little firecracker, you hear me?'

Keira doubted that Reed had picked up Jeff's comment – he was too busy chasing Wildflower around the corral. It was only when the farrier had packed up and gone, and Jacob had cornered the

Appie down the side of the barn, that events calmed down enough to deal with.

'Easy, easy,' Jacob soothed. He reached out and took up the end of the trailing rope.

Wildflower watched him warily. She breathed heavily, there was sweat across her chest and under her belly.

'No one wants to hurt you. You're going to do just fine.'

Cool! Keira loved her dad's gentle way with even the wildest, craziest horses – how he soothed them with his voice and his actions so that they quit struggling and looked to him to tell them what to do.

'Thanks,' Reed said, abruptly taking the rope from Jacob. 'I don't know why she acted crazy,' he muttered, red in the face and in a hurry to leave. 'I guess now Dad will have to make a few phone calls.'

'At least one of which will be to say sorry to Jeff for the hole in his van,' Jacob pointed out.

'Yeah, and to find a guy who knows how to fit shoes on her.' Reed was tightening Wildflower's cinch and the Appie was backing off, stressed all over again. As her rider stepped into the stirrups, she danced sideways and threw her head backwards.

'Take it easy,' Jacob advised.

Keira opened the corral gate to let Reed and Wildflower out on to the Low Ridge trail.

'And truly, Reed, I meant what I said earlier,' Jacob called after them. 'Bring Wildflower to Black

Pearl. Leave her with me for a few days and I won't charge you a cent.'

'Thanks again,' Reed said, frowning from under the peak of his cap. 'But I can handle this myself, Mr Lucas. Wildflower might give me a fight, but I'm the one who's going to win in the end, you can bet your life.'

CHAPTER THREE

'Reed's a great rider.' Brooke stuck up for their neighbour as she and Keira rode the trail. It was a week after the farrier fiasco and Keira had heard through her dad that Reed was still having problems with Wildflower.

'Brooke and I ran into Reed's dad at the tack store yesterday,' Jacob told Keira as he led Sasha out of the round pen and into the barn. 'Tom was buying a stronger bit for the Appaloosa. He said he was beginning to wish he'd never bought her over from Texas, but Reed won't give up on her. He's dead set on winning that fight he spoke about.'

'Hmm.' For once, Keira couldn't find a lot to say. But she thought plenty. And now she was out riding with Brooke, she shared her worries for poor Wildflower.

'Sure, Reed's good. He's been riding since he was two years old. But he doesn't know how to be gentle with a pony – not like Dad.'

Brooke disagreed. 'Don't be fooled. Reed acts tough, but he's not really. He has a good heart.'

'You didn't see him with Wildflower last Saturday.' Keira looked ahead to a flat, square outcrop of rock on the horizon. It was Navajo Rock – a favourite place where the girls would dismount to give Red Star and Annie a rest. 'The way he acted just made her more stressed.'

'So, he's not perfect.' Brooke clicked her tongue to set Annie into a trot up the hill. 'Maybe he was nervous having Dad around. Maybe he tried too hard to get it right.'

Keira trotted then loped to keep up. 'Are you kidding? Reed didn't listen to a word Dad said!'

'He's proud.' The wind was in Brooke's hair and blowing hard against her red padded jacket. She gave Annie her head and let her lope to the rock. 'He would hate it that Wildflower acted up in front of you all.'

Keira rode Red Star harder. The two ponies ran easily side by side. 'So how come you like Reed Walters so much all of a sudden?' she grinned.

'I don't!' Brooke shot back, her face suddenly as red as her jacket. 'He's a great rider, is all I'm saying!'

And she urged Annie on, as if beating Keira and Red Star to Navajo Rock was the only thing on her mind.

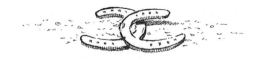

Brooke and Keira dismounted and tied Annie and Red Star to nearby pine trees. They sat on top of the flat rock, gazing down into the next valley. In the distance they saw a horse and rider heading their way.

'Guess who!' Keira said with a giggle, and she nudged Brooke with her elbow.

Blushing again, Brooke recognised Reed and

Wildflower. 'Don't say a word!' she warned.

Once Reed was within earshot, Keira scrambled down the rock to say hi. 'How's Wildflower doing?' she asked eagerly.

'Good.' Quickly Reed dismounted. 'Tuesday I got her some shoes and I've been riding her hard ever since. Today we were out at Sharman Lake. Hey, Brooke, how are you doing?'

'Good.' Trying her best not to show she was feeling shy, Brooke came down the rock after Keira. 'I heard about your new pony. She's real pretty.'

'Totally,' Keira agreed. She'd forgotten how beautiful the Appie was, and how nervy. Right now, for instance, she was dancing on the spot, putting in a small buck every now and then as if she wanted the saddle off her back.

'I'm taking her to the Ranch Rodeo at the Flying J,' Reed told them. 'I reckon she can win the barrel racing.'

'When is that?' Keira asked.

'Wednesday. Why? Are you planning to enter Red Star?'

'Maybe.' Keira hesitated. The Flying J was an hour's drive across country and she would have to ask her mom and dad.

'How about you and Annie?' Reed asked Brooke.

'We don't do rodeo,' Brooke answered. 'Maybe I'll come and watch you and Keira battle it out.'

'So what do you reckon, Keira? You think you can beat us?'

'What I think is – it's way too soon for you to

enter Wildflower,' Keira told him straight. 'You need to get to know her first.'

Reed shook his head. 'She's a great rodeo pony, believe me. She can stop and turn on a dime. She can lope from a standing start. You want to see her in action?'

Without waiting for an answer, he stepped back into the saddle. 'Come on, you two, I'll show you.'

So Brooke and Keira cut short their break and remounted their ponies. Soon the three of them were picking their way between trees and thorn bushes down into the valley where they'd first spotted Reed.

'You see that clearing?' he asked, pointing to a four hundred metre space in the valley bottom. 'And you see the pointed rock at the far end?'

The girls nodded.

'We race to it, turn them around and race back – OK?'

Keira was the first to say yes. Brooke's answer came more slowly. 'Yeah, but we need to take care,' she pointed out. 'There are a couple of fallen trees in the way, and the ground is pretty rough.'

'Wildflower can jump the logs, no problem,' Reed grinned. He lined them up at an imaginary start line and asked them if they were ready. 'Go!' he cried.

Keira felt Wildflower explode ahead of her. She'd covered ten metres before Red Star even began. Likewise, Annie was already way behind.

'Go, Red Star!' Keira urged.

Her pony launched himself after Reed and

Wildflower. His long stride ate up the ground and soon he was gaining on them, swerving around small boulders and coming up to the first log that got in their way. Keira felt Red Star gather himself up and soar through the air. She lifted herself out of the saddle and leaned forward. Whoosh! They made it over the log.

Now Reed touched Wildflower with his spurs. The Appie picked up more speed, head straining forward, mane and tail flying in the wind.

Keira didn't have to use spurs to get top speed out of Red Star. By the time they reached the rock they drew neck and neck with the leaders. But Reed rode tight around the marker, turning rapidly and streaking ahead again.

'No problem Red Star – we can catch them!'

Keira wouldn't give in. She was hard behind Wildflower, aware that Brooke and Annie had fallen well behind.

But boy, the Appie was fast. She jumped a log and forged ahead until Keira and Red Star put on a final burst of speed. In the end, the two ponies crossed the finish line together.

'Yee-hah!' Reed reined Wildflower to a halt, took off his cap and

38

slapped his pony's neck with it. 'That was cool!' he cried.

'Good boy, Red Star!' Keira leaned forward to pat his neck. Then she turned to watch Brooke bring Annie over the line.

'What did I say? Isn't she neat?' Breathless and grinning broadly, Reed let his pony prance and crow-hop on the spot. 'And wait until Wednesday – Wildflower will beat everyone in sight!'

'Dad, can I take Red Star to the Ranch Rodeo at the Flying J?' Keira had picked her moment. It was late Sunday afternoon and the sun was setting behind the Black Pearl mountains. Jacob was working quietly in the arena with Sasha.

'When is it?' he asked, beckoning for her to join him.

'Wednesday. Reed is taking Wildflower.'

'Really?' Jacob sounded a little surprised. 'Heck, yeah – I guess I can trailer you out there.'

'Thanks, Dad!'

'I can take along some chinks I made for Reed's dad.' In his spare time, Jacob made leather chinks and chaps – the leg protectors that cowboys strap around their waists and wear over their thighs. Keira's dad's chinks were made from fancy tooled leather with long fringes and were much in demand from his friends and neighbours. 'Hey, Keira, would you step up into the saddle?' he asked.

She nodded eagerly, guessing that it would be the

first time that Sasha had felt the weight of a rider on her back and knowing this was special. As Jacob stood at the filly's head and held her steady, she eased herself cautiously into the stirrup, leaned forward and let her body rest across the smooth saddle.

Beneath her, Sasha shifted her weight nervously.

'OK, throw your leg over,' Jacob instructed. Nothing about him gave off any sense of danger or tension.

Slowly, slowly, Keira slid her leg across the colt's back. Smoothly she sat upright.

'Good girl!' Jacob breathed. Then he handed the reins to Keira and stood back.

Keira sat totally quiet. She breathed deeply, evenly – wanting Sasha to believe that having a rider in the saddle was the most natural thing in the world.

And it was. They took a step forward, then another. Keira sat upright, perfectly balanced. She walked Sasha around the arena. As the sun disappeared behind the mountains, she saw the landscape soaked in a pearly dusk light.

'Perfect,' her dad said from across the arena.

And it was – being at Black Pearl Ranch, training colts, spending all her time with ponies – life for Keira was perfect.

CHAPTER FOUR

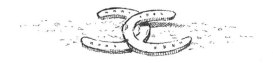

The Flying J Rodeo fell during the week of the October holiday, giving Keira and Red Star plenty of time to practise.

'You lucked out on the weather,' Brooke commented on the Monday afternoon as she watched Keira line up a row of blue plastic barrels in the arena. 'They forecast three days of sunshine.'

Keira nodded. 'Mom says she'll find the time to

come and watch on Wednesday, so we'll all be there.'

'Better get in some training if you want to beat Reed on Wildflower,' Brooke grinned, breaking off to answer a call on her mobile phone. 'Hey, Reed,' Keira heard her say as she went to fetch Red Star from the corral.

Soon, Keira and Red Star were weaving in and out of the line of barrels at full gallop. The pony kicked up dirt as he flew round the obstacles, making the tightest turn at the far end then racing back again. 'Brooke, can you time me?' she called as they got ready to start over.

Brooke was still busy on the phone. 'Later!' she replied.

Just then, Allyson came out of the tack room. 'I'll do it,' she offered.

'Ready – go!' Keira and Red Star set off, getting closer to the barrels to save time, Keira's leg almost brushing against them as they galloped by. She made the turn then headed for home.

'Forty-eight seconds!' Allyson told her. 'But I reckon you can still shave a couple of seconds from that time.'

'OK, let's take a rest,' Keira told Red Star, walking him over to where her mom and sister stood.

'Reed is complaining that Wildflower is cinchy,' Brooke was telling Allyson. 'He was asking me what to do about it.'

Allyson thought for a while. 'Well, if a pony gets mad when you tighten her cinch, maybe she's telling you that you need to let the cinch back out a notch or two. Or maybe there's pressure on her spine from the saddle. Did Reed check it out?'

'He said he went through everything, even put an extra blanket under the saddle – Wildflower still acted up.'

'From what your dad tells me, being cinchy is the least of that pony's problems,' Allyson sighed, giving Red Star's nose a quick stroke. 'So he's forecasting that Wednesday at the Flying J is going to be interesting.'

'Let's wait and see,' Brooke insisted. 'I reckon Reed knows what he's doing, whatever you all say.'

Tuesday was bright, cold and sunny just like they said. In the morning Keira worked with her dad and Sasha in the arena, bringing the colt to the point where she was almost ready to go home to Jim Peynton and his son.

'Good job!' Jacob told Keira as she neck-reined Sasha towards the middle of the round pen and pulled her up dead in the centre. They'd been working for thirty minutes and the little pony hadn't put a foot wrong.

Keira was ready to keep going, but suddenly Allyson came running out of the house with some news. 'Reed called. He's out at Dolphin Rock with Wildflower. They found an injured deer.'

Straight away, Keira slid from the saddle and led Sasha out of the arena. She tied her to the nearest rail then ran to join her mom and dad.

'Reed says, can we take the trailer up to the rock

and bring the deer back here?' Allyson explained. 'It's injured pretty badly. His dad's not home but he says he can't leave it out for the coyotes.'

Jacob nodded. 'Sure we can help,' he agreed.

Quickly he and Keira jumped into the trailer and headed out on the Jeep trail, taking a left fork away from Low Ridge and driving uphill and across country to reach Dolphin Rock, where they soon spotted Reed and Wildflower waiting for them.

Jacob drew up at a safe distance. For once, Keira noticed, Wildflower wasn't acting up, but standing perfectly still as if keeping guard over something that lay half hidden behind a thorn bush.

'Don't scare him – stay back,' Reed warned. 'He's lost a lot of blood so he's pretty weak.'

'What do you want us to do?' Jacob asked.

'We need to carry him into the trailer, but we don't want to spook him.' Slowly Reed walked Wildflower around the injured animal.

Keira held her breath. She could see the deer's antlers and part of his head, noticing that he tried to raise himself when Reed let his pony move in too close. But the stag was too weak to stand and he had to let Wildflower advance even closer, until she drew near enough to

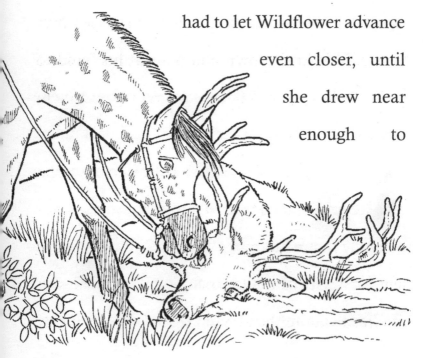

lower her head and nuzzle the deer's face.

'Who'd have thought that Wildflower would be this calm?' Keira muttered.

'Ponies know when another animal is in serious trouble,' her dad said. 'And the deer senses that Wildflower won't harm him.'

'OK, come closer,' Reed called to Keira and Jacob as he slid from the saddle and stooped over the stag. He knelt down and put out his hand to stroke his face, with Wildflower standing over them both, still keeping guard.

As Keira scrambled up the hill with her dad, she felt a lump rise in her throat. What if the deer was too badly injured to move? What if he died before they got him back to the ranch? And when she saw him, his beautiful head lying in the dirt, his great, dark eyes half closed and his sides heaving as he struggled for breath, she felt a sharp stab of fear.

'Where's the wound?' Jacob asked, kneeling beside Reed.

'In his shoulder – see!'

There was a dark red patch on his pale brown fur, a stream of blood, and another crimson patch on the ground. Straight away Jacob took off his neckerchief and rolled it into a pad which he pressed against the wound.

'Hold this in place,' he told Keira. Then he instructed Reed to raise the deer's head. 'I'll take most of the weight. Ready?'

The stag kicked his legs and made a feeble attempt to resist.

'Hush, lie still!' Keira whispered as she pressed

down on the pad and tried to stop the bleeding. 'How did this happen?' she gasped.

'Maybe he ran into a thicket and spiked himself on a broken branch,' her dad suggested. 'Who knows? OK, now we carry him down to the trailer. Watch your step, Reed. Good girl, Wildflower, you stay close by!'

It seemed like an age but finally they carried the deer into the trailer and laid him on a bed of straw. The frightened deer once more tried to stand.

'I know – it's dark in there and it doesn't feel good,' Jacob muttered. 'Reed, try loading Wildflower into the trailer to keep him calm.'

No sooner said than Reed was leading the Appie into the trailer and bolting the door behind her. Again, Wildflower, calm as anything, seemed to know exactly what she needed to do.

Then Jacob, Reed and Keira climbed into the cab and they drove slowly downhill, avoiding the worst bumps on the Jeep trail, all holding their breaths and hoping that it wasn't too late.

CHAPTER FIVE

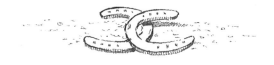

'Reed and Wildflower saved a stag's life!' Keira burst into the kitchen to tell Brooke the latest news. 'They found him up by Dolphin Rock. He'd lost a lot of blood. Dad's with him in the stable, giving him a shot of antibiotics …'

'Whoa, slow down!' Brooke pleaded. She logged off from the school project she was working on at the kitchen table and reached for her fleece jacket.

'You say Reed did this?' she asked, hurriedly

following Keira across the yard.

'And Wildflower. She was amazing! She stayed with the stag in the trailer. You wouldn't believe how sensible she acted.'

The two of them entered the barn and half-ran down the central aisle to the stable where Reed and Jacob were working on the injured stag. Wildflower was with them, standing quietly in the corner, keeping a wary eye on the girls.

'How's he doing?' Keira wanted to know. The stag still lay on his side, but his breathing was easier and his eyes wide open.

'Good,' Reed reported. 'I spoon fed him with water while your dad brought the medication. All he needs now is a shot of Bute to kill the pain.'

'Plus plenty of peace and quiet,' Jacob agreed,

finishing his task and asking Reed to lead the Appie out of the stable. 'We'll leave him here overnight – wait for him to regain his strength.'

Once more Wildflower acted grown-up and sensible. She simply lowered her head to breathe softly over the stag's face then allowed herself to be led quietly out of the barn.

'Totally amazing!' Brooke whispered once they were gathered in the corral. She stroked Wildflower's neck. 'She's like a different pony!'

Reed smiled. 'I knew she'd come right before too long.'

'Good job,' Jacob told him. 'You too, Keira.'

Keira knew she'd done very little. 'You're totally cool!' she whispered in Wildflower's ear.

'The thing is, Wildflower and me – we bonded

out there by Dolphin Rock.' As he mounted his pony and got ready to ride home, Reed tried to explain. 'I remembered what you told me, Mr Lucas – about getting her to accept me and all. I reckon it happened when we worked together to save the stag.'

Jacob nodded. 'Good job,' he murmured again.

'So tomorrow we go to the Flying J and prove we're a team.' Reed turned Wildflower towards Low Ridge. 'Keira, you and Red Star had better watch out – Wildflower and I plan to fly around those barrels and take first prize – you wait and see!'

Next morning before dawn, the stag was up on its feet in the stable next to Red Star's. Its antlered head peered over the door as Keira turned on the barn light and walked down the aisle.

'Hey!' She greeted the deer with a glad smile. 'Someone feels good this morning!'

As she passed by, Red Star stretched out his neck and took a nip at the sleeve of her jacket. What about me?

'Hey, you – I didn't forget about you!' she laughed. 'Dad told me to clean up this guy's wound before I do anything else.'

So she went into the deer's stable, steering clear of the sharp antlers and hoping that he wouldn't spook so that she could get close enough to clean the gash in his shoulder. He shifted nervously back into the corner of the stable, watching Keira's every move.

She waited a while then she had an idea. 'Red Star, why don't you tell him not to be scared?' she said as she went next door to fetch him into the deer's stall. She waited while her pony nosed about in the blood-stained straw bed then ambled over to the wild creature in the corner. Soon the deer stopped shaking and began to sniff curiously at Red Star's feet.

'They're iron shoes,' Keira explained as she moved in with an antiseptic wipe. 'You won't have seen them close up before.'

The deer hardly seemed to notice as she cleaned his wound. When she'd finished, he breathed deeply then strolled over to the water bucket by the door.

'Red Star wears shoes like that to protect his

hooves. And they help him not to slip. He'll sure need them today for the barrel racing.'

'Yackety-yack-yack!' Brooke laughed at Keira as she stuck her head over the stable door. 'Mom says breakfast is ready,' she told her. 'So quit talking to the animals and come eat!'

The Flying J was sixty minutes' drive through Forestry Commission land. It sat tucked under the foothills of the Black Pearl range, close to fast-running Bear Creek on the only flat grassland for miles around.

'Ranch Rodeo – Wednesday 25th October', Keira read the big red letters on the banner stretched across the gateway as her mom drove over the cattle guard. The track leading to the ranch was lined with trailers like their own – mostly battered and rusty, but with one or two sleek new models belonging to the wealthier ranchers in Matheson County. Seeing them gave Keira a knot in her stomach.

'Nervous?' Allyson asked.

Keira nodded, glad that the adult rodeo events came before the junior barrel racing because it would leave her plenty of time to unload Red Star and get him ready. She especially looked forward to watching her dad ride Misty in the cutting competition.

'I see a place to park!' Brooke pointed to a space close to the ranch house and Allyson pulled over. Soon the back door of the trailer was open and

Misty and Red Star were stepping out.

'Hey, Jacob, how are you doing?' 'Allyson, good to see you!' 'Hi, girls – gee, you've grown!' Neighbours from all around the county came to greet them, including Tom Walters, who wanted to pay Jacob for his new leather chinks. Brooke and Keira soon spotted Reed beside the Walters' trailer and went to talk with him.

'Hey, Reed. How's Wildflower?' Brooke asked.

'See for yourself,' he said proudly, stepping aside.

'Wow!' Keira was impressed. Reed had brushed Wildflower's cream and brown coat until it shone. Her dark mane and tail flowed like silk. 'You even polished her hooves!'

'She looks gorgeous,' Brooke added.

'Too gorgeous,' Keira frowned, dashing back to

Red Star to groom him and bring him up to Wildflower's level.

Meanwhile, Jacob got Misty ready for the cow cutting contest and when his turn came, Brooke, Keira and Allyson went to the arena to watch.

They threaded their way through a crowd of about two hundred people until they found a good viewing point. 'Now I'm nervous!' the girls' mom admitted, showing them her crossed fingers.

'Don't be!' Brooke and Keira chorused then grinned. They both knew how good their dad was at cutting out one cow from a bunch of twenty and roping it with his lasso.

'Dad is the real deal,' Brooke added, turning her head towards the entrance and waiting for him to ride Misty into the arena.

There were five other riders before him – each one at ease in the saddle and pretty good with cows. They rode close to the bunch, chose one and cut it loose from the herd. Then they circled their lassos above their heads and went in with the rope. Sometimes it took two or three attempts, but in the end they roped it.

Keira studied the printed list. 'Dad's next!' she exclaimed.

Sure enough, Jacob rode Misty into the arena, his face half hidden by the broad brim of his best black Stetson. He had his rope looped neatly over his saddle horn and he wore a pair of his own fancy, fringed chinks.

Behind the arena fence, Keira felt proud – he looked so calm and easy out there, and Misty brushed up as good as any cow horse around.

Over the far side, a cowboy opened a gate to a bunch of small black cows, all jostling each other and mooing loudly as they entered the arena. They stuck together and trotted clumsily until they met a barrier, then they lowered their heads and turned, trotting aimlessly on.

Jacob held Misty back until the cows got used to their surroundings. He took his time, picked one out in his mind's eye, lifted his rope from the saddle horn and waited for his chance.

The cows bunched together and picked up speed as Jacob rode Misty straight at them. He raised his lasso and whirled it above his head. Then he threw.

Keira heard the whizz of the rope through the

air. She bit her lip and watched it land right on target, over the cow's head and around her neck.

'Good job!' The crowd cheered and applauded.

Jacob leaned back in the saddle and Misty stood firm. The rope tightened, the cow strained to break free, but she had no chance – the contest was over.

Keira clapped along with the rest of the crowd. It looked like her dad was in line for a prize. But now, she needed to focus on Red Star and the barrel race.

'Time to saddle up,' her mom told her.

They hurried back to the trailer where Red Star was tethered and waiting patiently.

'Ready?' Keira asked him as Allyson tightened his cinch and Brooke checked his bridle.

Her pony stamped his front foot.

'That's a yes!' Brooke grinned, holding his head while Keira stepped into the saddle.

Close by, Reed was preparing Wildflower for the contest. 'Stand!' he told his pony while Tom Walters tightened the cinch.

Wildflower tensed up and kicked out, stepping sideways as she felt Reed's weight in the stirrup. But she settled once her rider was firmly in the saddle.

Together Reed and Keira walked their ponies towards the entrance to the arena.

'What do you reckon – how fast can you go?' Reed asked Keira, keeping Wildflower on a tight rein.

'Faster than you!' was all she would say. She

looked ahead, her back straight, head raised and focusing forward. Red Star stepped out towards the opening gate, eager to begin.

'Number 8 – Keira Lucas on her strawberry roan pony, Red Star!' the voice on the loudspeaker announced.

'Let's go!' she whispered.

They trotted through the gate then once around the arena until they came to the start line.

The guy on the loudspeaker made his final announcement: 'Keira and Red Star, your time starts ... now!'

And Keira and Red Star launched themselves towards the barrels.

CHAPTER SIX

R ed Star set off at a fast lope and Keira steered him around each barrel, reining him first left and then right, putting on pressure with her legs.

'That's quick!' someone in the crowd said. 'She's a neat rider,' someone else added.

Keira heard none of it – she was focused on the last barrel in the line, ready to turn Red Star and head for the finish line. She reined him hard to the right.

'Oh!' the crowd gasped. They saw one of Red Star's reins break loose from the bridle and drag uselessly along the ground.

Uh-oh! Keira felt the metal clip snap and saw the rein fall. *Now how did she steer?*

In the audience, Jacob, Allyson and Brooke groaned in unison.

But brilliant Red Star didn't miss a beat. OK, so his bridle had broken, the bit had slid out of his mouth and one rein was trailing in the dirt. So what? He turned and galloped back, in and out of the row of barrels, racing like the wind.

'Wow!' 'Look at that pony go!' 'That's amazing!'

Keira held her breath as Red Star raced for the finish.

'In spite of the glitch, Keira and Red Star made

a time of forty-three seconds!' the announcer declared. 'That makes them the fastest so far!'

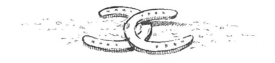

'You're a total star!' Back by the trailer, a breathless Keira threw her arms around her pony's neck. 'You did that all by yourself – you're unbelievable!'

'The metal ring snapped clean in two,' her dad said as he examined the broken bridle. 'But trust Red Star to keep on going.'

Meanwhile, back in the arena, the announcer introduced Reed and Wildflower.

'Next up is a new combination – number 9, Reed Walters and his Appaloosa, a little beauty named Wildflower. Reed, the time to beat is an excellent 43 seconds …'

'I have to watch this!' Keira exclaimed, leaving Red Star with her dad and rushing back to the arena just in time to see Wildflower prance uneasily through the gate. The Appie seemed on edge, ears flat and eyes rolling, most likely scared by the sea of faces and the loud voice on the sound system.

'Reed and Wildflower, your time starts … now!'

Reed pressed his spurred heels against her side and Wildflower reacted as if she'd been shot. She exploded straight up into the air, her back humped, head down and all four legs locked at the knee.

'Oh!' A gasp went up from the crowd as she landed and bucked again, twisting as she rose into the air and kicking out with her back legs as she hit the ground. Up in the saddle, Reed was thrown about like a rag doll.

Keira gripped the fence rail, hardly able to look. Poor Wildflower was crazy with fear, whipping her head this way and that until she tore the reins out of Reed's hands. He grabbed for the saddle horn but it was too late. His pony rocked back on her haunches and then did something that a horse hardly ever does – she rose high on her hind legs, arched her spine and jerked her whole body straight backwards.

'Jeez, no!' 'Is she crazy?' Seeing what was about to happen, people in the crowd started to climb the fence into the arena. A cowboy ran in through the gate and sprinted to try and break Reed's fall.

Up Wildflower went on to her hind legs, arching her back and flipping over so that her rider had no chance. Reed tipped out of the saddle, bounced back over her haunches, and had already hit the ground when Wildflower crashed down on top of him.

Keira's heart missed a beat. The crowd fell silent.

For the few seconds that Reed lay trapped under his pony, time seemed to stand still.

Then Wildflower rolled to one side and got to her feet, men were running, the crowd was buzzing again.

Get up, Reed! Keira prayed silently.

He lay on his back totally still, eyes closed, one arm flung wide.

'Get up!' Keira breathed.

He didn't move. His dad reached his side and dropped to his knees beside him.

'Don't move him,' someone warned.

A first aider ran in and waved everyone except Tom Walters back. 'Give him space! Fetch the ambulance!'

'What's happening?' Brooke cried, suddenly appearing at Keira's side. It took time for her to take in the scene – Reed lying unconscious, Wildflower loose in the arena, reins trailing as she bucked and writhed.

Seconds later the paramedics raced in and unrolled a stretcher. They took instruments out of their packs and fixed a brace around his neck. As they bent over Reed, their backs to the crowd, Keira lost sight of her injured friend.

And now Wildflower was breaking into a flat gallop, careering round the arena, heading for the open gate.

'Stop the pony!' Keira heard her mom's voice shout a warning.

Wildflower's hooves pounded the ground, foam gathered at her mouth.

A cowboy ran across the exit route, flinging both arms wide. The pony swerved past him and galloped on. She was thundering down the alleyway between two sets of rails, her only thought to get as far away from the noise and action as she could.

Carefully the paramedics lifted Reed on to the stretcher and strapped him tight. Madly Wildflower struck out for freedom.

The last Keira saw of Reed was when the ambulance door closed behind him.

She turned and looked for Wildflower – saw her clear the Flying J cattle guard at full gallop and keep on going, heading for the foothills of the Black Pearl range.

CHAPTER SEVEN

'It happened the way you predicted,' Allyson told Jacob later that evening.

The Lucas family was back home, the ponies and the injured deer all safely fed and watered. A red, setting sun slid slowly behind the dark, jagged horizon.

'What do you mean?' Jacob asked. He sounded tired.

'You told Reed not to push that Appaloosa too

hard too soon,' Allyson reminded him. 'They never had time to bond.'

'But Wildflower was so good with the stag,' Brooke protested. 'She did everything right – Reed was praising her and telling her how good she was.'

'That's true.' Her dad got up from the table and turned off the porch light, sighing as he went. 'But it takes more than one good experience for a pony to really trust her rider. Scratch the surface and Wildflower was still unhappy with her new surroundings, her new owner and all.'

Keira sat at the table letting the conversation drift on. Had Reed been too hot-headed, or was Brooke right to stand up for him? Keira didn't know. But she was sure it had turned out badly, with Reed in the hospital at Elk Springs and Wildflower lost in

the mountains.
Picturing the
pony now – out
there alone in
the cold and
dark – she
shuddered.

'You OK?'
her mom asked,
leaning across to
put an arm around Keira's shoulder.

Keira shook her head. 'What's going to happen
to Wildflower?' she asked in a small, scared voice.

Allyson frowned. 'She has a couple of options.
One is to stay up in the mountains overnight and
come down to the Flying J in the morning, once

she gets hungry. Another is to head for home.'

'But the Flying J is miles and miles away from the Three Horseshoes,' Keira whispered. 'Through pine forest and across high mountain passes. And it's dark!'

'Ponies see pretty well in the dark,' her mom reminded her. 'And they have an amazing homing instinct. Don't be surprised if Wildflower turns up at the Walters' cattle guard first thing tomorrow morning.'

'I hope!' Keira said, crossing her fingers.

'I have some news from the hospital,' Jacob said as he put the phone down. 'Tom is with Reed, waiting for him to regain consciousness. The doctors ran a brain scan. They say he took a hard knock to the back of his head. He's covered in cuts and bruises, but nothing is broken, thank God.'

'And so to bed,' Allyson decided, rounding the girls up and shooing them through the door and up the stairs. 'There's no point us sitting around stressing over the pair of them. The best we can do is to get some rest.'

All night Keira tossed and turned in her bed. It was one thing for her mom to sound calm and confident over Wildflower, but another for Keira to stop worrying.

There are bears in the mountains, she thought as she stared at the ceiling. *And packs of coyotes. Plus, a pony could slip and fall down the mountain. Wildflower could get stuck in a gulch or lost in a blizzard – anything!*

The longer she thought about it, the more she worried.

She'll hate being out there alone! This was the idea that stuck in Keira's head and played itself over and over. Wildflower all by herself in the dark, spooking at the least little sound, growing colder and colder as the night went on.

The hours crawled by, and still Keira couldn't sleep. She was glad when the first fingers of grey light crept into the sky and she could roll out of her crumpled bed to get dressed.

She was first down the stairs, first to pull on her boots and zip up her jacket, first to venture out into the icy morning.

'Where are you going?' Brooke appeared at the

head of the stairs when she heard Keira moving around in the kitchen. She was still in her pyjamas, her dark hair tousled, her eyes full of sleep.

'Out to the barn,' Keira replied softly. 'I want to check on the stag.'

She stepped out on to the porch then across the yard, through the corral and into the barn. The big door creaked as she closed it behind her. An owl flew low down the central aisle and out of a window at the far end. Keira walked on, feeling calmer in the safe, silent space and glad to see Red Star poking his head over his door, ready to greet her.

'Hey, I hope you're taking care of our deer,' she murmured, peering into his stable. Sure enough, the stag lay quietly in a bed of clean straw, his dark, almond-shaped eyes enormous in his delicate face. When he saw Keira, he rose to his feet.

'You're looking good,' she told him without going in. Something her mom had mentioned made perfect sense – 'Take care not to handle him too much. Remember he's a wild animal. He won't want the scent of humans on him when he takes off back into the forest.'

The stag tilted his head to one side as if curious, but not afraid.

'Red Star is looking out for you,' she murmured, stroking her pony softly on his muzzle. 'He takes care of me all the time. You can totally trust him.'

Keira stood a while gazing at the stag. Then she had an idea. 'Come on,' she told Red Star, opening his door and letting him step out of the stable. 'Let's get your tack. We're going on a trail.

'Mom says there's a chance that Wildflower will head for the Three Horseshoes,' she explained after she'd saddled Red Star and they set out along Low Ridge. 'The only problem is – Tom is with Reed in the hospital, so there's no one home.'

Red Star looked straight ahead, trotting steadily. By now, the sun had risen behind Dolphin Rock and cast a reddish light over the hills. Frost covered the ground in a sparkling white carpet.

Keira felt happier now that she was in action. She began to look to the right and left of the trail, up the hills and across the creek, searching for any movement amongst the bare willows growing at its edge. She spotted three mule-deer beyond the trees, heads raised, listening and looking intently.

'Have you seen a runaway Appie?' she wanted to ask.

The deer grew nervous and bounded away between the pine trees.

Soon Keira and Red Star reached the Walters' place. There were cows in the corral – hundreds of them surrounding a row of big iron racks, trampling and jostling to get at the best feed. There were more mule-deer on a rock on the slope above the ranch house, even a coyote slinking out of sight as Keira and her pony trotted into view.

But there was no Wildflower waiting for them, her head anxiously raised, her reins still trailing along the ground, her saddle and saddle pad perhaps pulled to one side, her coat covered in sweat and mud.

'I'll take a closer look,' Keira decided, riding into the yard beside the ranch house then dismounting. She left Red Star tethered to a rail and went walkabout by the frozen creek.

Her boots crunched in the thick frost. She stooped beneath low branches and stepped clumsily through tall bushes, pushing them aside. At every step she expected to see a shape, to spot a movement, hear a soft whinny or the snort of a pony who had galloped through the night to come home.

But there was nothing by the stream or higher up the hillside when she looked there. There were no telltale hoof prints in the frost, no droppings –

nothing to show that Wildflower had been there.

Keira searched for a full hour then went back to the corral. Red Star raised his head hopefully but she shrugged and went on into the Walters' barn, where she found grain pellets and fed them to old Duke and Tom's black horse, Thunder. She gave them water and told them Tom and Reed would soon be home. She sighed as she said it, not really believing her own words.

Once she was sure that the two horses were safe and content, she went back to Red Star, mounted up and rode home to find her dad waiting for her in the corral.

Jacob didn't speak as she stepped down from the saddle. He didn't ask questions – he simply waited for Keira to explain.

'Wildflower didn't make it home,' she told him with tears in her eyes.

'You didn't find any sign?'

She shook her head. 'I looked everywhere.'

'Then she stayed in territory closer to where she ran away,' her dad decided. 'Nice try, Keira. I'm sorry you didn't succeed. Now come and eat.'

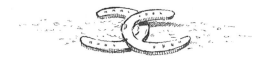

'You can't do anything on an empty stomach,' Allyson said firmly.

Still in her warm fleece jacket, and with her reddish-blonde hair arranged in two loose braids, Keira sat at the table and forced down her meal of bacon and eggs. When the phone rang, she almost jumped out of her seat.

Brooke ran to answer it and came back with a message. 'That was Reed's dad.'

Jacob, Allyson and Keira froze and waited for more.

'Reed woke up,' Brooke explained, her face flushed and her voice breaking with relief. 'But he only remembers part of what happened.'

'Well, thank God he's regained consciousness.' Allyson picked up the plate she'd almost dropped when Brooke announced the news.

'Mr Walters says Reed can't recall what spooked Wildflower, or how come he fell off,' Brooke went on. 'But he does remember one important thing.'

'Which is?' Keira urged.

'The last thing Reed saw before he fell unconscious was Wildflower taking off through the arena gate.'

'And?'

Brooke turned to their mom. 'He wants us to visit him at the hospital. Mr Walters says Reed needs to talk to us real bad.'

CHAPTER EIGHT

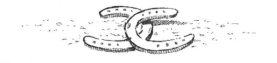

'We only permit two visitors at a time,' the strict nurse at the nurses' station told the Lucas family when they arrived at the hospital in Elk Springs. 'Reed is still pretty weak. We don't want to overtire him.'

'So you two go ahead,' Jacob told Keira and Brooke. 'Your mom and I will wait here.'

The girls went on tiptoe down the shiny corridor to the end room where they found Tom Walters sitting at his son's bedside. Tom rose when he saw them and told them to come in.

'You have visitors, son,' he told Reed, backing out of the room to give Brooke and Keira time with the patient.

Brooke gasped and Keira frowned when they saw their buddy wired up to monitors and looking white as a sheet.

'Hey!' He made an effort to sit up straight and fix a grin on his face.

'Stay still!' Brooke said quickly as they sat at his bedside. 'Wow, you really took a fall!'

'Yeah, but nothing's broken. They're going to let me out of here as soon as they've finished taking pictures of my stupid head.'

'Yeah, your stupid head,' Brooke echoed. 'When

are you going to listen to good advice and not go

charging at barrels before your pony's settled in?'

'Hey, don't give him a hard time.' For once, Keira

was the one sticking up for Reed. 'Reed reckoned

Wildflower was ready. Look at the way she acted

around the stag.'

Reed sighed then shook his head. 'Ouch!' he

groaned. 'That hurt. It feels like I've got mushed-up

potato for brains.' He sank back against his pillow. 'Everything's still kind of hazy.'

'That's normal,' Brooke insisted. 'You had a ton of horse fall on top of you, remember.'

'I got Wildflower into the arena, didn't I?' Reed looked to Keira for an answer. 'You and Red Star went in front of us. You made a good time.'

Keira nodded. 'Red Star's bridle snapped but he went right on. He made me proud.'

'Yeah, I remember that now. And I know Wildflower was nervy the way she always is. Plus, I know she didn't like that big crowd – the noise set her on edge, her ears went back, her eyes started to roll. Maybe that's when I should have pulled her out of the competition.'

Neither Brooke nor Keira argued with this. They

sat quietly, realising that events were flooding back for him.

'Your dad was right,' Reed told them quietly. 'I pushed my pony too hard too soon. I was looking at winning the contest, whatever it took.'

'So we all make mistakes,' Brooke murmured more kindly.

There was an awkward silence, broken only by the bleeping of one of the machines. Then with a choking voice, Reed did his best to face up to his feelings. 'It's not that I don't care about Wildflower – I do! I know she's getting to like me and listen to what I ask her to do. She's real smart.'

'And pretty,' Keira added.

'And brave,' Brooke said.

They sat for a moment with the picture of the

Appie in their heads – her beautiful dark face and mane, her fine arched neck, her long legs, the lovely chocolate and cream colouring.

'I want her to love me back,' Reed confessed, his lips trembling.

'She will,' Brooke promised. 'When she comes home.'

'If she comes home,' Reed added in the quietest voice. 'I know she ran away. I see it as clear as you two sitting here. She took off for the hills.'

There was another silence that seemed to go on

and on before Reed looked from Keira to Brooke and back again. 'Find Wildflower for me,' he pleaded. 'Make sure she's safe and bring her back home.'

'I agree it's a race against time.' Allyson sat at the kitchen table listening to Brooke and Keira's pleas. 'You're right – the cold weather is drawing in and that's bad for any pony on the loose in the mountains.'

'But?' Jacob could hear the 'but' in her tone of voice. 'You don't think it's wise for the girls to ride up there and take a look?'

We promised Reed! Keira thought, holding her breath and biting her lip. *We told him we'd search!*

They'd been back from the hospital for a couple of hours, brought in the Black Pearl ponies from the meadow, done the barn chores and now sat opposite their mom and dad, explaining their plan.

'It may not be safe,' Allyson said. 'Brooke and Keira don't know the territory out at the Flying J. And there's the weather to consider.'

'Dad could trailer us over there first thing tomorrow morning,' Brooke insisted.

'I could do that,' he agreed.

'Red Star and Annie will keep us safe,' Keira said eagerly. 'They know not to try anything dangerous.'

'And I could spend time driving along the jeep roads in the area, stopping places and asking folks if they've seen a runaway Appaloosa,' their dad said thoughtfully.

'Yeah, Mom, please!' Brooke and Keira said together.

Allyson put her hands together and interlaced her fingers. She stared for a while at her palms. 'It's a deal…,' she agreed at last.

Keira and Brooke threw themselves at her and gave her a hug.

'… Provided you check in every hour or so with your dad,' their mom continued. 'Now you go to bed, get a good night's sleep and in the morning you fulfil your promise to Reed – you go out and bring Wildflower back home.'

Next morning Keira and Brooke got up together before dawn. They put on their boots and jackets and made ready to go out to the barn.

'Check on the stag while you're out there,' their dad called from the top of the stairs.

Out in the yard it was still pitch black – there were no moon or stars in the sky and a freezing wind swept down from the Black Pearl peaks. The girls hurried to open the barn door and reach for the light switch. At the end of the long aisle, sleepy ponies stuck their heads over their stable doors and whinnied softly.

'How's our stag?' Keira went right up to Red Star, pulled wisps of straw out of his mane and stroked his nose. Then she peered into the next stall. The creature that Wildflower had helped to rescue gazed peacefully back at her from his bed. 'Today we're riding out to find your missing buddy,'

Keira promised, turning to put a head collar on Red Star and lead him out of the barn. Brooke and Annie were already a few steps ahead.

'The stag's doing great,' Keira reported to their dad once they walked their ponies out into the corral.

He was there with the trailer, opening up the rear door and waiting for the girls to load Annie and Red Star. 'That's one piece of good news,' he said. 'Let's hope the rest of the day goes as smoothly.'

'Here – take these packed lunches.' Allyson had come out of the house with hastily made sandwiches, corn chips and an apple to eat on the trail. 'And remember, you girls ride together and you don't split up. Plus, you arrange with your dad when and where to check in with him and you stick to the plan.'

Keira and Brooke nodded and told her not to worry. Jacob was up in the cab, it was time to leave.

'Good luck!' their mom called. She stood and waved the trailer out of the yard, lit by the light

shining in the house porch, looking worried in spite of the smile and the wave she gave them as they left.

'Eleven o'clock!' Jacob said, tapping his wristwatch and making sure that Brooke and Keira understood. Then he handed over the map that they'd just finished studying. 'We meet by the visitors' centre out by Bear Creek. You got that?'

He'd parked the trailer in the yard of the Flying J after the long, bumpy journey over dirt tracks through National Forest land. As they'd driven, the invisible sun had risen behind thick clouds. By nine-fifteen they'd arrived, unloaded Annie and Red Star, saddled them up and were ready to ride.

'Got it,' Keira and Brooke chorused. With hope in their hearts and a vision of what Reed would say to them when they brought Wildflower home, they were eager to start.

'And don't try anything too western!' Jacob

warned, looking up at them as they stepped into their saddles. 'Meaning, don't take any risks up there.'

'We won't!' they promised.

They grinned and pointed their ponies up the trail, trotting them out through tall pine trees, up the first slopes in their journey into the mountains.

CHAPTER NINE

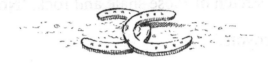

'Wow, this is wild territory!' Brooke sighed as she reined Annie to a halt under the shelter of some aspen trees.

She and Keira had ridden for almost an hour and it had been uphill all the way. The wind pushed against them, slowing progress, and clouds seemed to be dropping lower on to the mountains, turning the whole scene grey and dull.

Keira and Red Star joined Brooke under the

trees. 'There's no grass anywhere,' she muttered. 'Nothing for Wildflower to eat. And it's so cold!'

'We haven't seen a single sign of life.' Brooke wore a deep frown as she stared up the mountain, across a stretch of loose shale and rock. 'Not even deer or coyote.'

'So let's cut back down to Bear Creek,' Keira decided. 'Maybe Wildflower stayed where there's water.'

'And anyway it'll be time to meet Dad,' Brooke remembered, pulling the map from her pocket to check the route.

Both girls were glad to turn their ponies and head for more sheltered ground. They sat back in their saddles to ease the strain for Red Star and Annie on the downward track through pine forest towards the camp ground and their meeting place with Jacob.

Sure enough, there was the Black Pearl trailer with their dad standing beside the cab, waving to them as they drew near.

'Nothing?' Jacob called, reading their glum expressions.

Keira and Brooke shook their heads. They didn't dismount, but listened carefully to his own news.

'Me neither,' he sighed. 'It's like that pony vanished into thin air.'

'Who did you ask?' Keira wanted to know.

'I met a couple of Forest rangers – they didn't know anything. And there's a small ranching outfit down the creek from here. The guy there hadn't seen Wildflower either.'

As they talked, Red Star kept his head up, twitching his ears and listening intently. Once he even threw back his head and whinnied loudly, then stood as if waiting for a reply. The noise carried a long way but was greeted with silence.

'What do we do next?' Brooke asked as a pair of hikers arrived at the camp ground.

The hikers – a man and a woman dressed in knitted hats and heavy padded jackets – put their rucksacks on one of the picnic tables then waved at the riders and their dad.

'Have you seen a runaway Appaloosa?' Keira called to them. 'She's out on the mountain all alone. We're trying to track her down.'

The woman hiker walked quickly across. 'You know, maybe we did,' she told Keira. 'I said to my husband back there on the trail, I thought I heard a horse close by in a thicket of thorns and willows. I wasn't sure though. I mean, it's not what you expect to hear.'

'Where was that?' Keira gasped.

Brooke came to show the couple their map. 'Could you point to the place on here?'

The woman studied the map then prodded it with her finger.

'We were

coming along

the creek. It

was close to

where this

smaller creek

runs down to join

Bear Creek – right here!'

'Thanks!' For Keira and Brooke it was the first chink of hope they'd been given. They rode quickly back to Jacob and told him where they were headed.

'Let's go!' Keira insisted.

'Meet back here at one o'clock,' their dad told them. 'And remember – stick together!'

Red Star and Annie sensed the girls' excitement. They strode out along the side of Bear Creek, sometimes splashing into the water when the path was blocked by boulders and thickets. Their hooves knocked and crunched against the rocks on the bed of the creek. They kicked up spray and forged ahead while their riders looked left and right, expecting any moment to get a sighting of Wildflower.

But the first living thing they met was a hunter, standing by a pine tree, his gun over his shoulder.

'Whoa!' Keira told Red Star. She turned and pointed out the man to Brooke.

'What do we do? Do we ask him?'

'Sure.' Brooke rode right on up, even though the hunter was frowning and turning away. 'Did you see a runaway Appie?' she asked. 'Dark brown with cream markings, out here all alone.'

The man shook his head. 'Yeah, like I'm looking for an Appaloosa!' he grunted sarcastically. 'Will you quit making all that noise. You scared away my deer.'

Good! Keira thought. She hated the idea of any

of the beautiful creatures being harmed. And she took an instant dislike to the bad-tempered hunter.

He was about to walk away when he turned back. 'You'd better try higher up the mountain,' he muttered. 'I saw tracks up beyond the tree line, over in that direction.'

'Thanks!' Brooke was grateful and straight away turned Annie up the mountain.

Keira followed more slowly, thinking that maybe the hunter had sent them off in the wrong direction just to get rid of them. But what could they do? They had to follow his direction, just in case.

Once more Red Star and Annie worked hard to climb the steep slope. And now the clouds came rolling down the hillside, carrying the first snowflakes on the icy wind. The girls ducked their heads and pulled down the brims of their hats, feeling the flakes settle on their cheeks and melt.

'We have thirty minutes to scout the area beyond the tree line,' Brooke reminded Keira. 'Then it'll be time to turn around.'

Keira nodded. They were clear of the trees now, but not able to see far ahead because of the falling snow which settled quickly on the stony ground.

'The snow will soon cover Wildflower's tracks,' Brooke said anxiously.

'If there are tracks ...' Keira sighed. Then she shared her doubts about the hunter's advice with Brooke.

'Wait!' Brooke had glanced towards a group of pointed rocks to her left. Quickly she checked the map and decided that the feature was marked as Needle Rocks. 'That's good shelter in this kind of weather. Let me take a look.'

She set off without waiting for Keira, who spotted an equally likely refuge in the opposite direction. It was time for rapid action – the snow was getting worse and their dad would be waiting anxiously at the camp ground. So Keira pointed Red Star towards the boulder to her right and urged him into a trot. Willingly he carried on the search.

The boulder was further away than Keira expected, and the ground was tougher. Red Star's hooves lost their grip on the soft snow that had already fallen. He slipped and slid, regained his footing then tried again to reach the rock.

'One more time!' Keira whispered. The snow fell more heavily still, almost blinding her.

At last they reached their goal. Keira rode Red Star out of the wind, around the back of the boulder. *Please be there, Wildflower!* she prayed.

But there was nothing except a small black squirrel which scurried on to the top of the rock and out of sight. So Keira rode full circle and headed Red Star back the way they'd come.

But was it the right way? Already the blizzard

had covered their tracks and made everything look different. And the snow was falling so thick and fast that no way could Keira make out Needle Rocks. So she called out her sister's name.

'Brooke, where are you?'

The wind howled down the hillside and swept away her voice. There was no reply.

Red Star threw back his head and whinnied. Annie didn't answer.

'I guess it's this way,' Keira muttered, heading downhill and hoping for the best.

But then something happened. She heard a horse call from way up the mountain – a high, shrill whinny that Red Star heard too. He turned his head, pricked his ears and whinnied a second time.

Once more, there was a faint reply.

'Wildflower!' Keira gasped. Up there, alone in the winter storm. Lost. Scared.

'Hang on in there – we're coming!' she cried, turning Red Star back up the snow-covered hillside, heading way up into the wilderness.

CHAPTER TEN

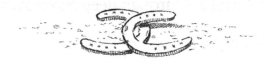

This was the worst storm Keira had ever ridden through. Huge snowflakes stung her cheeks; the freezing wind cut right through her thick jacket. Still she and Red Star pressed on up the mountain.

'Call again!' Keira whispered to her brave pony.

Red Star raised his head to whinny. From way up ahead came a faint reply.

'That's Wildflower – I know it is!' Keira steered

Red Star between some tall rocks, into a deep gulley, hoping to find an exit at the far end. But the gulley narrowed and came to a dead end of sharp, overhanging rocks and they had to retrace their steps. They trudged through deep snow back on to the exposed hillside.

Once more Keira felt the full force of the wind. It whipped Red Star's mane from his face and whirled snow into her eyes. She had to lean forward to stay in the saddle. And now even Red Star seemed to hesitate, turning his head towards her as if to say, *So which way do you want me to go?*

'I don't know!' Keira groaned. A loud voice inside her head was telling her to head back down the hill to find Brooke. 'Stick together!' Her dad's clear instruction came back to her, and she knew he was right. But she'd lost sight of her sister in an instant – one moment she and Annie were visible, the next they'd vanished. And now Keira was without a map, not knowing where Brooke was or how to find the camp ground by the creek. Neither did she know where Wildflower might have sought shelter from the storm. 'We're lost!' she whispered to Red Star.

He looked at her and pawed the snow. Then he tossed his head and turned to face down the snow-swept slope.

'I know! We should go down and find the others,'

Keira sighed. 'But what about Wildflower? We can't leave her here!'

Red Star pawed the ground a second time. *Let's go down!*

Keira shook her head. 'What do I tell Reed when we get back home without his pony? "We heard Wildflower in the distance but the storm was too bad so we came down without her. Sorry." That would break his heart clean in two.'

In spite of the tug on his reins telling him to stand still, Red Star took a step down the slope.

'You're not listening!' Keira pulled again on the reins. 'We need to go higher.'

Ignoring her, Red Star pricked his ears towards the valley bottom then let out a shrill whinny. He listened intently.

Keira listened too and heard the faintest reply. 'No, that's Annie calling back to you,' she guessed. 'Not Wildflower.'

This way! Red Star fought the bit and took another step down the hill. He whinnied again, heard another reply then carried on. He stumbled down an unseen hollow, lunged forward then hauled himself clear. Keira felt herself flung forward in the saddle then back again.

'Is this really what you want to do?' she gasped. Red Star never acted this stubborn. What had got into him? 'Oh!' Suddenly she got it. 'You think that's Wildflower calling to us? You reckon she came down the mountain to find us!'

Of course! Why didn't I trust you to know what to do? Keira slackened the reins and gave Red Star his head. He plunged on through the snow, following sounds that Keira couldn't hear, down the slope through the blinding storm.

Down they went until they came to a steep dip and the sound of water cascading over rocks. Keira leaned forward in the saddle to take in the icy banks of a fast running stream. 'This must be the creek the hikers mentioned. If we follow this down we reach Bear Creek.'

Stopping by the waterfall, Red Star shook snow from his mane and sighed. He looked up and down the hillside, flicking his ears this way and that. Then he gave a loud snort. *Take a look over there by the overhanging rock!*

Keira peered from under the brim of her hat through the thickly falling snow. Under the rocky shelter she spied a large animal, its head raised and listening to their approach. Gradually she made out what it was.

'Mule-deer,' she murmured, her heart thudding with disappointment.

The female deer sprang out from beneath the overhang and pretty soon two more followed. They bounded through a snow drift, plunging deep then

raising themselves out, scrambling at last on to a more solid ridge.

Keira closed her eyes and sighed. 'Nice try,' she told Red Star. 'But that's not who we're looking for.'

He snorted again, kept his ears pricked towards the overhang and took a few more steps forward. *Look again!*

'What?' Keira muttered. 'There's nothing there. Come on, let's go.'

Red Star refused to move.

She took one last, despairing look.

Deep in the shadows something moved. The wind whirled snowflakes in a crazy dance and gradually the creature materialised. It peered out from under the rock, its head hanging low, its dark mane caked with frozen snow – a picture of pure misery.

'Wildflower!' Keira breathed. She blinked then looked again, to double-check that she wasn't seeing a ghost. It really was the missing Appaloosa with her saddle still in place, though one stirrup was missing, and with reins hanging loose and trailing in the snow. 'You poor thing, you must be freezing!'

At the sound of Keira's voice, Reed's Appie backed deeper into the shadows.

'It's OK, we're here to take you home. We've got hay in the trailer and a nice warm stable back at Black Pearl Ranch.'

The runaway pony stared warily at Red Star and his rider. She trembled from head to foot, seemingly ready to burst out from under the

overhang and take flight.

'Red Star, you've got to let her know that we're her friends,' Keira whispered. 'If she runs away again, we've got no chance of catching her in this storm!'

So Red Star walked steadily forward – not too fast, not too slow – with his eyes and ears fixed on poor Wildflower, willing her not to run.

The trembling Appie stretched her neck towards him and flared her nostrils. *Friend or foe?*

'Good boy,' Keira told Red Star. 'Easy does it.'

They were five, maybe six paces away from Wildflower, stepping under the overhang, edging closer. Red Star held Wildflower's gaze until they were by her side. Then Keira leaned out of the saddle and eased herself forward to take hold of

Wildflower's trailing reins. She grasped the thin leather strap and held it tight.

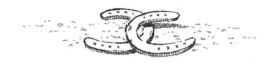

'It was like magic!' Brooke told Keira. 'Annie and I came straight down off the mountain and we found Dad at the camp ground. I told him the whole story – how we got separated on the mountain, how I yelled and yelled your name but you didn't reply. He was ready to set off on foot to find you …'

'… When there you were right before our eyes!' Jacob had just finished loading the three ponies into the trailer. He'd dried off Red Star, Annie and Wildflower and made sure they had something to eat.

Brooke grinned from ear to ear. 'The snow was

easing by then and we saw you and Red Star leading Wildflower down the side of the creek. At first I thought I was dreaming. I want to know how you did that.'

'I did what Mom and Dad always tell us to do – I trusted my pony,' Keira explained. She felt warm tears of relief trickle down her cheeks. 'Red Star knew what he was doing from the get-go. He tracked down Wildflower and made sure she didn't spook. She let me grab her rein and that was it – job done!'

When Red Star heard her say his name he looked her way and snickered. Keira smiled and took the apple out of her packed lunch. She offered him a bite. 'Don't be greedy,' she murmured. 'Leave some for Wildflower and Annie.' Soon all three

ponies were munching happily.

'You did a good job,' Jacob told her as he closed the trailer door. 'You kept your head and your nerve.'

In spite of the cold, Keira felt a warm glow of satisfaction. She peered in through the small window at Wildflower safely tethered between Annie and Red Star. 'Let's go home,' she whispered softly.

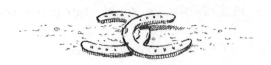

That night Keira fell into bed exhausted. She slept right through until her mom tapped on the door at seven-thirty and came into the room.

'Did you sleep well?' Allyson asked as she sat on the side of the bed.

'Uhhh,' Keira sighed. She rubbed her eyes and sat up.

'Your dad plans to set our stag free before breakfast. I thought maybe you'd like to be there.'

Keira was suddenly wide awake. 'Don't let him do it without me,' she gabbled, already out of bed and half way into her jeans and sweatshirt. She pulled on her socks and ran downstairs after Allyson.

'Boots, jacket, gloves, scarf,' her mom reminded her. 'It's bright but chilly out there.'

'Yeah, see you!' Still zipping up her jacket, Keira broke out of the house and across the snowy yard. She burst into the barn and ran down the centre aisle.

'Whoa!' Her dad was in the stall with Ruby and Toots. He poked his head over the door when he heard Keira's hurried footsteps.

'You didn't let the stag go yet, did you?' She stopped to draw breath by Red Star's stall, giving him a quick pat before she went on. 'And how's Wildflower? Where's Brooke? How's Reed? Did we hear from the hospital?'

'Whoa!' Jacob said again. 'One question at a time is all I can deal with this early in the morning.'

It was then that Brooke's head appeared over the

door of a stall. 'The stag's still here,' she told Keira. And Wildflower is doing good – see for yourself.'

Keira took a deep breath and went to look. She found Wildflower in the stable next to Ruby's, standing quietly at her feed bucket and scarcely raising her head when Keira peered over the door. *Don't bother me while I'm eating* was the message.

'First thing this morning I checked her over,' Jacob said as he came to join Keira. 'I reckon I found out why she's been hard to handle.'

'So?' For a moment Keira was worried.

'Wildflower has a lot of tension down her spine, and a sore place just behind her withers – maybe a trapped nerve. So when the weight of the saddle is on, she feels the pressure, and it gets worse every time Reed tightens her cinch.'

Keira nodded thoughtfully. 'And can you untrap the nerve?'

'Not me personally, but I know a horse-doctor guy who can. I'll speak to Reed's dad about it next time I see him.'

'You hear that?' Keira spoke softly to Wildflower who had finished her feed and come to the door. 'No more nasty back pain. How about that?'

Wildflower nuzzled Keira's hand then pricked her ears at the sound of a car pulling up in the yard.

'Were we expecting someone to call?' Brooke left the stag's stall and hurried to the barn door, where she met her mom.

'We have visitors,' Allyson announced, calling them all outside.

'Hey, Reed!' Brooke was the first to run to greet him and his dad. 'They let you out of the hospital!'

Soon the whole family crowded around the car. Reed sat in the passenger seat looking pale and anxious.

'He has to take it easy until the cuts and bruises heal up,' Tom Walters explained. 'But he wouldn't let me drive home until we dropped in here.'

'Keira found Wildflower up on the mountain – did you hear?' Brooke knew that Allyson had called Tom as soon as they'd unloaded the three ponies from the trailer the day before. 'How much did your dad tell you? Did he say there was a snowstorm going on up there and Keira got lost but Red Star found Wildflower sheltering under an overhang ...'

'Let the boy breathe,' Allyson insisted. She

opened the car door for Reed and helped him out.
'Wildflower is just fine,' she told him. 'Are you OK
to wait here while we bring her out?'

Reed nodded. His face was still tensed up into a
frown.

'We'll be back,' Keira promised.

She and Brooke ran into the barn, whispering
together and nodding their

heads. Reed
stood next to his
dad, hands in his
jean pockets, his
jacket zipped up
to the chin. All
eyes were fixed
on the barn door.

They seemed to wait a long time until they heard movements in the dark entrance.

The stag's magnificent antlers appeared first, then his beautiful head. He stood framed by the door, sniffing the morning air. He glanced at the bunch of people gathered in the yard then turned to focus on the snow-laden pine trees growing on the slopes rising out of the empty meadow. It was a white world. The sky was blue.

With a sudden surge of energy, the stag bounded across the corral and clean over the fence. He was healthy, he was free.

With a cautious smile Reed watched the stag leap towards the forest. Then he turned back towards the barn.

It was Keira who led Wildflower into the corral.

The Appie pranced at her side, head up, ears pricked forward, her long black mane lifted by the breeze. When she spotted Reed, she immediately set off high-stepping towards him.

Keira held on to the lead rope and ran alongside. She saw Reed's eyes grow wide and his smile soften to one of pure joy. 'Take her,' she murmured, putting the lead rope into his hand.

'Hey, girl!' Reed whispered. He leaned his head against Wildflower's cheek and spoke softly into her ear. 'I was scared I'd never set eyes on you again. But the girls found you and brought you back!'

Wildflower snickered and nudged Reed's shoulder with her nose.

'I reckon she's glad to see you,' Brooke told him.

Reed put both arms around his pony's neck.
'Likewise,' he murmured with tears in his eyes.

Right there and then Reed and his dad had made
a deal with Jacob. They would leave Wildflower at
Black Pearl Ranch and let Jacob call in the horse
doctor to fix her back.

'After that, will you guys work with her in the
round pen?' Tom had asked. 'Put in some basic

training, ready for Reed to ride her when he's healed?'

Keira had almost jumped for joy. She'd run straight to the barn to tell Red Star the latest news.

Now, later that morning, Wildflower was cosy and warm in the stables and Keira was hard at work as usual.

'Bring Sasha in from the meadow,' her dad instructed. 'Jim Peynton will be here to collect her straight after lunch.'

'And take extra feed,' Allyson said. 'The ponies will need it in this weather.'

Keira ran out to the meadow with a huge bundle of sweet-smelling alfalfa. She opened the gate and was soon surrounded by Red Star, Annie, Captain and Misty. Ruby, Willow and their foals were close behind, while Sasha hung back.

'Hey, there's enough for everyone!' Keira laughed, handing out the hay. She saved some specially for Sasha and for Toots and Spider. The foals tugged it from her hand then ran off, kicking up snow. Full of fun, they bounded and leaped straight in the air, landing knock-kneed and tumbling in the white powder, rolling and getting

up on their spindly legs to canter again.

'Cute!' Keira said to Red Star. She put her arm around his neck and looked up at the sparkling white peaks of the Black Pearl range. She thought of their stag roaming the forest, of Wildflower safe in their barn, and knew once again that life didn't get any more perfect.

Keira's home is **Black Pearl Ranch**, where she helps train ponies – and lives the dream ...

Black Pearl Ponies

MISS MOLLY

Sable Lucas's parents plan to give her a surprise birthday gift – a beautiful sorrel mare called Miss Molly! They allow Keira's dad three short weeks to train the nervy pony.

Soon Sable is all set to meet Miss Molly, but the great day goes horribly wrong. Why does the pony spook big-time? Keira turns detective to find out.

Keira's home is **Black Pearl Ranch**, where she helps train ponies – and lives the dream …

Black Pearl ponies

STORMCLOUD

Stormcloud is a crazy ex-rodeo pony that can never be tamed. Or so everyone believes. But Stormy's new owner promises Keira that if she succeeds in re-schooling him and selling him on, she can keep the cash!

Keira jumps at the challenge. Will kindness and patience be enough, or has rodeo cruelty soured Stormy for good?

Black Pearl Ponies

SNICKERS

Keira is thrilled when two high bred colts – Vegas and Snickers – arrive at the ranch, but she soon falls out with the owner's spoiled son, Rex.

It's bad enough that Rex breaks her dad's rules, but when he mistreats poor Snickers Keira faces a tough choice: confront Rex and lose valuable business, or keep quiet and risk Snickers coming to serious harm?